Margaret Yordon
&

Addie's Adventures at the North Pole

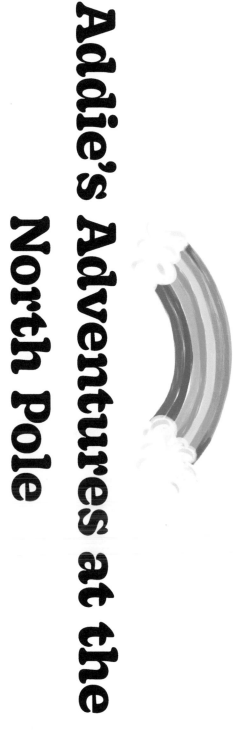

The Awakened Press

www.theawakenedpress.com

For information about special discounts for bulk purchases, please contact The Awakened Press at books@theawakenedpress.com.

The Awakened Press can bring authors to your live event. For more information or to book an event contact books@theawakenedpress.com or visit our website at www.theawakenedpress.com.

Cover and book design by Kurt A. Dierking II

Illustrations and cover art by Lucia Benito
www.tuolvidastodo.com

Printed in the United States of America
First The Awakened Press trade paperback edition

ISBN: 979-8-9870434-0-0

Addie's Adventures at the North Pole

The Awakened Press

This Book Belongs to:

From:

Date:

SANTA'S TOY WORKSHOP

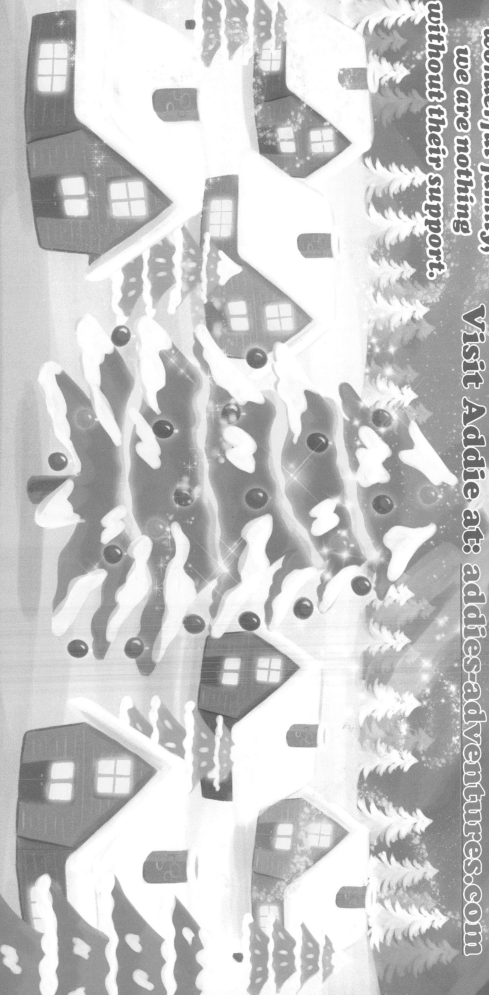

Addie's Adventures at the North Pole

By: M&S Gordon

Illustrated by: Lucia Benito

Dedicated to our wonderful family; we are nothing without their support.

Visit Addie at: addies-adventures.com

Addie loves adventures and traveling everywhere

She floats in her
hot-air balloon

across

sea,

land,
and

air

Today Addie's adventure is at the North Pole so cold

A snowy magical village sparkling
in silver and gold

Addie and Lexy float over
Santa's village below

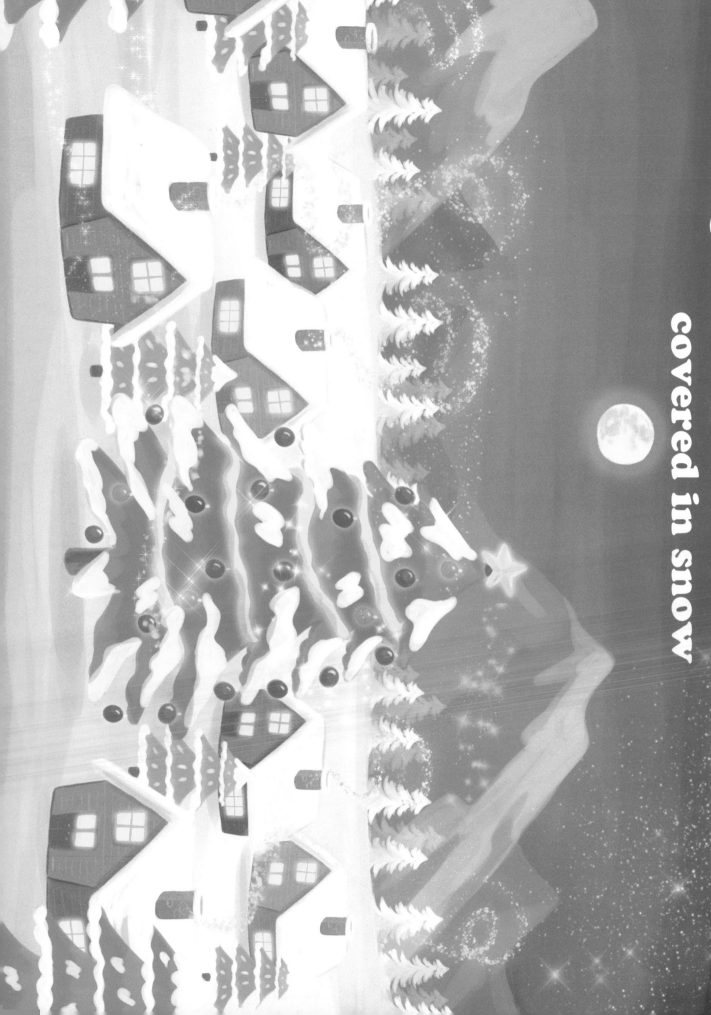

Looking in wonder at sparkly lights all covered in snow

Christmas Eve will
soon be near

The time to help
Santa is here

Addie came to help Santa get
ready for his big day

When Santa travels the world in his shiny red sleigh

Addie is here to help Santa, the elves, and reindeer

Who were hard at work making toys through the year

Addie helps them make toys and then wraps them with care

Adding magical bows that send peace
and love through the air

Santa's village is such a wonder so bright

Seeing toys everywhere is an amazing sight

The toys and packages are stacked up to the sky

Santa's sleigh and reindeers
are now ready to fly

Today Addie

helped Santa

build so many

wonderful toys

Making Christmas so special for all the little girls and boys

The North Pole was so much fun today,
and Addie smiled from her balloon

This adventure was amazing, and Addie made a wish to come back soon

Addie is on to another adventure!

CPSIA information can be obtained
at www.ICGtesting.com
Printed in the USA
BVHW091829281122
651958BV00001B/2